When Sheep Sleep

by Laura Numeroff
illustrated by David McPhail

SCHOLASTIC INC.

New York Toronto London Auckland Sydney
Mexico City New Delhi Hong Kong Buenos Aires

When you can't fall asleep,
Then try counting sheep!

But what do you do if the sheep are asleep?

Count deer in the forest
Instead of the sheep.
Together all nuzzled,
They don't make a peep!

Count cows in the meadow
Instead of the sheep.
But under the moonlight,
They've fallen asleep!

Count pigs in the pig pen
Instead of the sheep.
They wiggle in mud,
And snore in a heap.

Count puppies on pillows
Instead of the sheep.
All cozy and cuddled,
They curl up to sleep.

Count birds in the treetop
Instead of the sheep.
Dreaming high in their nest,
They can't hear a cheep!

Count cats on the sofa
Instead of the sheep.
They're all purring softly,
and snuggled asleep.

Count bears in the cave den
Instead of the sheep.
Their mom watches closely,
Their safety to keep.

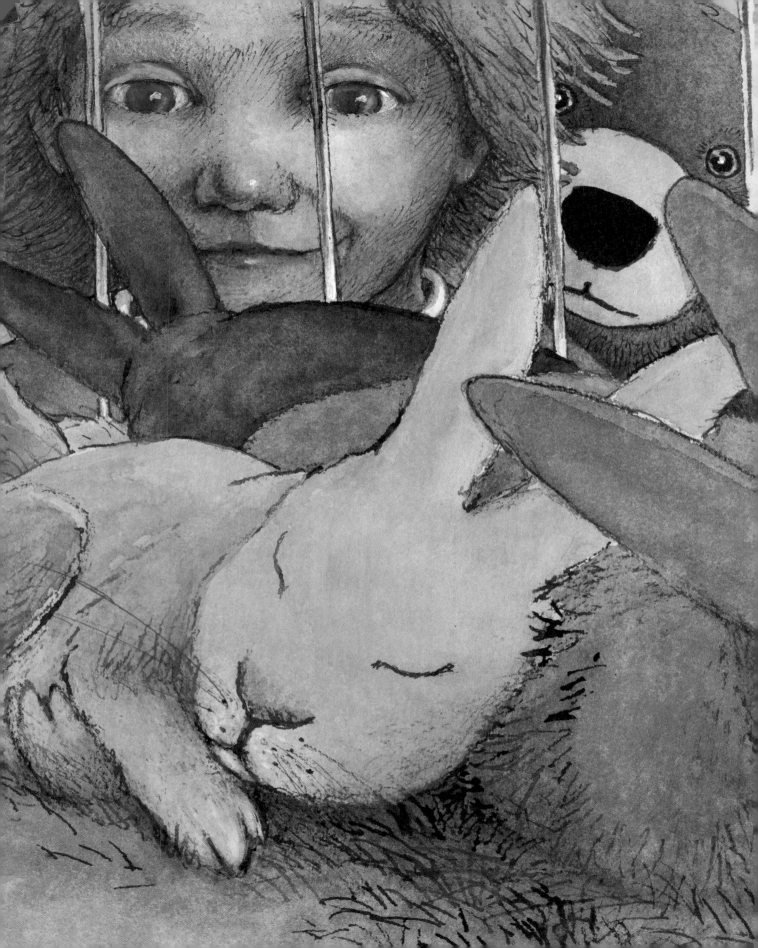

Count rabbits in hutches
Instead of the sheep.
Their noses still twitching,
They lay fast asleep.

With all of this counting
You feel like the sheep.
At last you are ready
To drift off to sleep!

For Daniel Lawrence Kleeger, with love
—L.N.
For Laura and Tamar, true believers
—D.M.

ISBN-13: 978-0-545-03595-8
ISBN-10: 0-545-03595-3

Text copyright © 2006 by Laura Numeroff.
Illustrations copyright © 2006 by David McPhail.
All rights reserved. Published by Scholastic Inc., 557 Broadway, New York, NY 10012,
by arrangement with Abrams Books for Young Readers, an imprint of Harry N. Abrams, Inc.
SCHOLASTIC and associated logos are trademarks
and/or registered trademarks of Scholastic Inc.

12 11 10 9 8 7 6 5 4 3 2 1   8 9 10 11 12 13/0

Printed in the U.S.A.   40

First Scholastic paperback printing, November 2008

Editor: Tamar Brazis

Designer: Edward Miller